For Tiggy
M.M.

For Sophie and Bailey
L.C.

First published in 2001 in Great Britain by
Gullane Children's Books

Text © Miriam Moss 2001
Illustrations © Lynne Chapman 2001

This 2008 edition published by Sandy Creek
by arrangement with Gullane Children's Books
185 Fleet Street, London, EC4A 2HS, United Kingdom

All rights reserved. No part of this publication
may be reproduced, stored in a retrieval system,
or transmitted in any form or by any means,
electronic, mechanical, photocopying,
recording or otherwise, without prior
written permission from the publisher.

Sandy Creek, 122 Fifth Avenue, New York, NY 10011

ISBN-13: 978-1-4351-0925-4

10   9   8   7   6   5   4   3   2   1

Printed and bound in Indonesia

The Grumpy Day

Miriam Moss
Illustrated by Lynne Chapman

SANDY CREEK

Smudge jumped out of bed.
"Ow!" she said, stubbing
her toe on the chair.
"Oh, no!" she cried as
she opened the curtains.
It was pouring with rain.
Now she would be
stuck inside all day.

Smudge got dressed in a fed up sort of way.
Then she looked in the mirror.
Every single button was buttoned up wrong.
"Oh, no! No! No!" she shouted angrily.

"Good morning," smiled Stripe.
"Bad morning," said Smudge.
"What's the matter?" asked Stripe.
"Everything," replied Smudge grumpily.
"Have some breakfast," said Stripe.
"I don't want any," Smudge said.

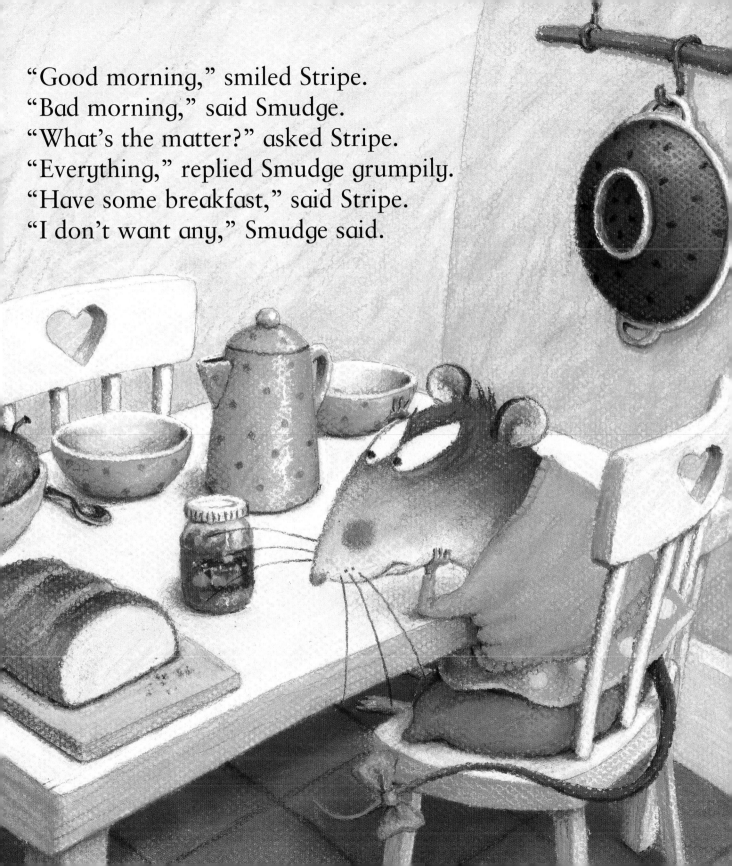

Stripe cut some bread. "What should we do today?" he asked.
"Not answer any more questions," said Smudge rudely.
"What is the matter?" said Stripe, "Can I help?"
"No, you can't," Smudge said, looking mad.

"If you're going to be rude," said Stripe calmly,
"perhaps you'd better go and do it somewhere else."
"I will go somewhere else," Smudge cried, stomping
out of the room, "and I won't come back ever!"

SLAM! went the back door as Smudge left home.

She marched across the lawn, down the path towards the river.
The rain trickled under her collar and down her neck.

Smudge stood by the river for a long time
watching the water flow by and feeling miserable.

Suddenly Goose paddled up.
"Hello, Goose," said Smudge. "I'm glad to see you."
"Are you?" said Goose. "Why?"
"Because I've just left home," announced Smudge.
"Goodness!" said Goose. "Forever?"
"Forever," said Smudge.

Smudge wiped the rain from her eyes.
"Well, why don't we go and play in
your treehouse," Goose suggested.
Smudge smiled. "Okay!" she said.

Soon Smudge forgot about being grumpy
and miserable because she was having
such a great time with Goose.

Hare and Mole rowed around the bend in the river.
"Ahoy there!" shouted Hare. "Come and
play pirates with us."

Smudge and Goose climbed aboard.
"Smudge has left home," said Goose.
"Oh dear!" Mole gasped, looking worried.
"Forever?" asked Hare.
"I think so," said Smudge.

They had a great time playing pirates, and somehow
Goose always ended up walking the plank!
Then it began to get dark.

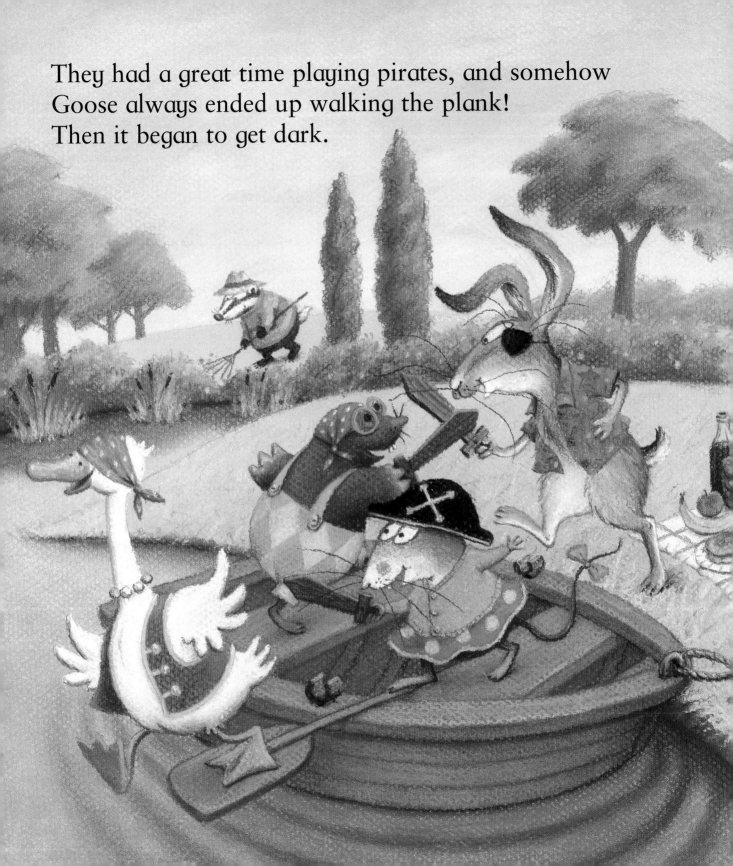

"Smudge, why don't you go home, just for tonight?"
suggested Mole, as they rowed home.
"I don't think I can. I told Stripe I wouldn't
ever come back," explained Smudge.

"Then you'll have to stay the night in your treehouse!"
cried Hare, "I bet you're brave enough."
Smudge looked very unsure.

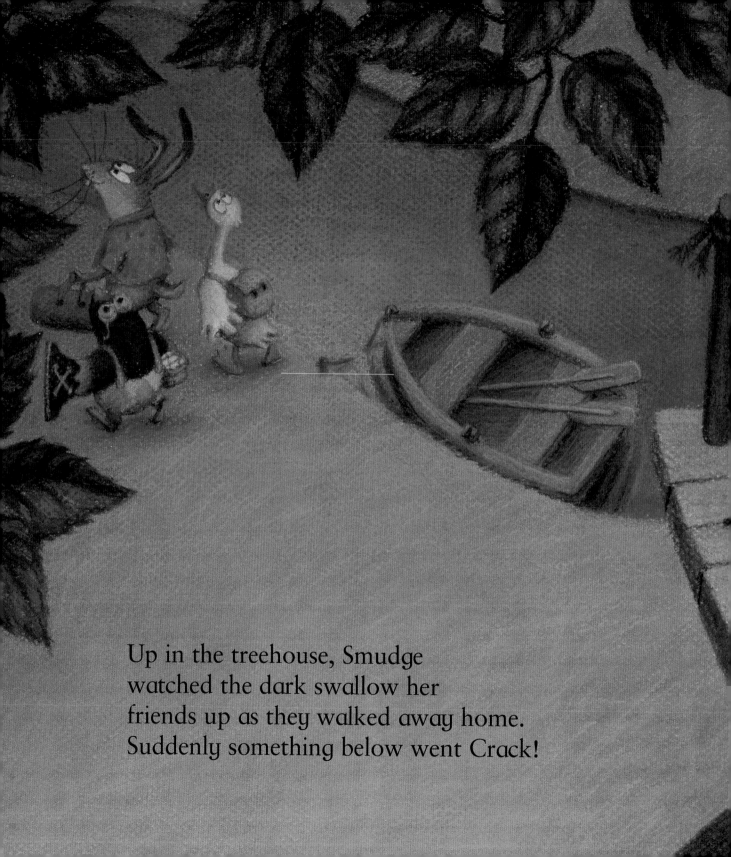

Up in the treehouse, Smudge
watched the dark swallow her
friends up as they walked away home.
Suddenly something below went Crack!

Smudge froze. Something
was coming to get her!
She shut her eyes . . .

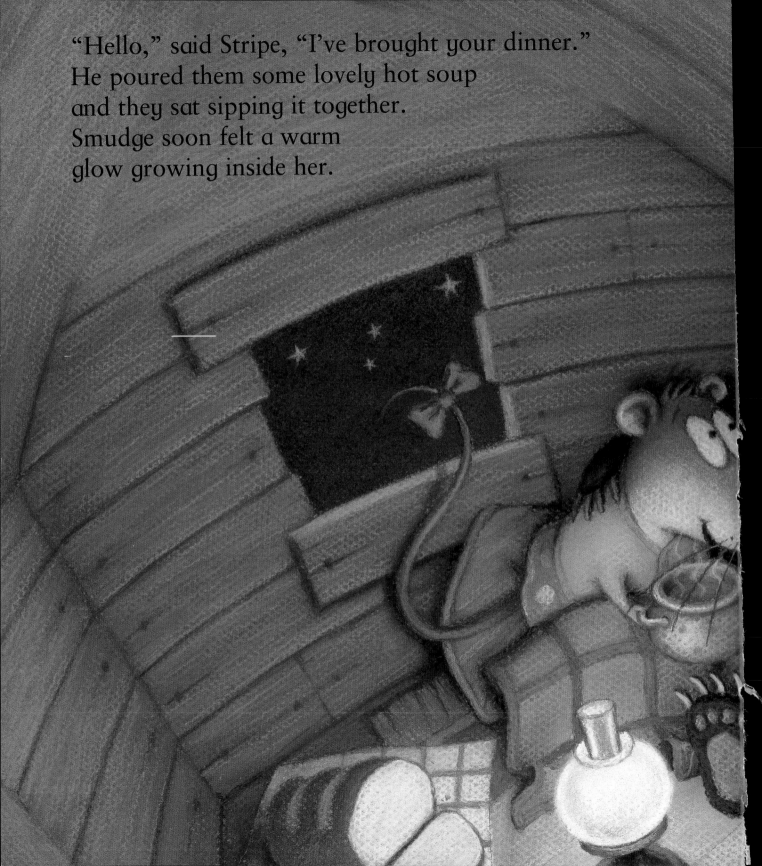

"Hello," said Stripe, "I've brought your dinner."
He poured them some lovely hot soup
and they sat sipping it together.
Smudge soon felt a warm
glow growing inside her.

"I was grumpy this morning, wasn't I?" Smudge said.
"Yes, but everyone is sometimes," Stripe said gently.
"I didn't run far away," continued
Smudge, "because I missed you."
"I missed you too," smiled Stripe.
"When we've had dinner,
shall we go home?"